The Wind and the Sun argued.

"I am the strongest!"

shouted the Wind.

“I am!”

glinted the Sun.

"I bet I can get
that
man's
coat
off!"

boasted
the Wind.

He tried hard,

but the man just shivered
and held on to his coat.

"I can do better,"
flashed the Sun.